A note to readers about Sniffing and **BARKING**

I'm as pleased as a puppy you've decided to read this book, so before you begin, I want to tell you something important.

This is a book about being happy.

It is as much a game as a story. The best way to enjoy it is by joining in the sniffing and barking. Try not to be shy.

Imagine that today is a lovely happy sunny summer day and you're a dog and you've just been let off your leash.

I find the best thing is to run about a bit first. On all fours.

 Sniff eagerly, without thinking. Explore the world with your nose.

Hey, can anyone smell sausages?

WOOF! WOOF!
Bark because you're happy.

WOOF! WOOF!
Bark the tune of "Happy Birthday."

WOOF! WOOF!

Isn't barking easy-peasy?

Warning! Don't play this game with real dogs. They get too excited. Play only with other pretend dogs. Like yourself.

Now turn the page and let's all get on with . . . Polly

Molly

WOOF

WOOF

For Lucky, for luck
D. L.

For Richard, Molly, and Max
C. H.

Text copyright © 2000 by David Lloyd
Illustrations copyright © 2000 by Charlotte Hard

First U.S. edition 2000

Library of Congress Cataloging-in-Publication Data

Lloyd, David, date.
Polly Molly Woof Woof : a book about being happy / David Lloyd ; illustrated by Charlotte Hard.—1st U.S. ed.
p. cm.
Summary : The happy barking of Molly and her dog friends spreads happiness to their owners.
The reader is asked to bark and sniff at various points in the story.

ISBN 0-7636-0755-X

[1. Dogs—Fiction. 2. Happiness—Fiction. 3. Literary recreations.] I. Hard , Charlotte , ill. II. Title.
PZ7.L774Po   2000
[E]—dc21   99-34808

2 4 6 8 10 9 7 5 3 1

Printed in Hong Kong

This book was typeset in Highlander, Johann, and Tempus Sans.
The illustrations were done in pencil, ink, and watercolor.

Candlewick Press
2067 Massachusetts Avenue
Cambridge, Massachusetts 02140

Polly Molly Woof Woof

A book about being happy

David Lloyd   illustrated by Charlotte Hard

CANDLEWICK PRESS
CAMBRIDGE, MASSACHUSETTS

A funny thing happened
on one lovely happy
sunny summer day
when Polly took Molly
to the park.

When Polly let Molly off the leash, Molly ran a short way out into the open, then she threw back her head and began to **bark** in a great **loud** voice.

This is your first chance to join in the barking.

Give it a try. Let's hear you. I think it's best to start as loudly as you can.

WOOF!
WOOF!
WOOF!

When Molly began to bark,
soon another dog came running,
a smaller, more **bouncy** dog
than Molly, and Molly stopped
barking. Molly and the little bouncy
dog began sniffing the air
and each other.

Now join in the
sniffing, if you like.

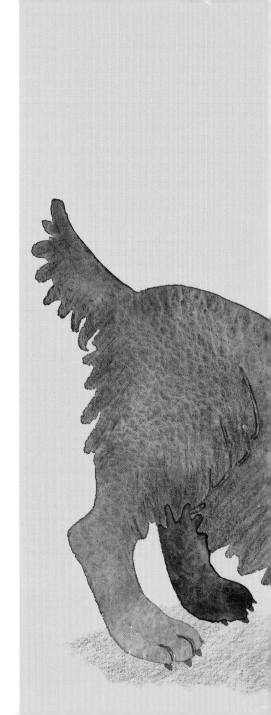

Then Molly in a great **loud** voice and the little bouncy dog in a little **bouncy** voice began to **bark** together.

Try both kinds of barking:
the loud woofs
and the bouncy ones.

Make both kinds sound
as happy as you can.

WOOF! WOOF! WOOF!

Soon two other dogs came running, one **sausage** dog and one rather **sad**-looking dog.
Molly and the little bouncy dog stopped barking.
All the dogs began Sniffing the air and each other.

Just look at all
these dogs, and
sniff just like they do.

Then Molly in a great **loud** voice and the little bouncy dog in a little **bouncy** voice and the sausage dog in a **sausage** voice and the rather sad-looking dog in rather a **sad** voice began to **bark** together.

Try the sausage barking.
Try the rather sad barking.
Don't forget to be happy.

Soon more dogs came running, one with a **fierce** face (but really she was very gentle) and one **thin** dog and one **fat** dog. Molly and all the other dogs stopped barking. All the dogs began sniffing the air and each other.

Now the sniffing's getting really busy.
The dogs are busy sniffing.
I'm busy sniffing.
Are you busy sniffing too?

sniff!

Then Molly in a great **loud** voice and the little bouncy dog in a little **bouncy** voice and the sausage dog in a **sausage** voice and the sad-looking dog in a **sad** voice and the dog with a fierce face in a **fierce** voice and the thin dog and the fat dog in a **thin** voice and a **fat** voice began to **bark** together.

WOOF!

WOOF!

What a noise!
What a racket!
Good boy!
Good girl!
Now this is what
I call happy.

I don't know what happiness smells like, do you?

Maybe to a dog it smells like bones
  and grass
    and sausages.

Maybe to you or me it smells like plums
  and bright flowers
    and pencils
      and the seaside
        and something warm and soft like a baby.

No, I don't know exactly
what happiness smells like,
but all those dogs obviously do, don't they?

And when I join in their sniffing

sniff! Sniff!

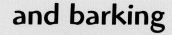

and barking

WOOF! WOOF!

I can certainly feel
what the happiness felt like
on that lovely happy
sunny summer day, can't you?

And it makes me want to
burst out laughing—which
brings me right back to the story....

Polly began to **laugh** and so did all the other people who had brought their dogs to the park on that lovely happy sunny summer day.

You can laugh too if you like, loudly or bouncily or sausagely or sadly or fiercely or thinly or fatly or whatever way you like best.

At last the people who were laughing started **calling** their dogs who were barking...

Molly!

Lucky!

Bob!

Sally!

And when the dogs
heard their names, they took
one last sniff
of the air and each other...

now I hope that you too will take
one last sniff...

and barked **one**
last enormous
bark together...

Then Polly took Molly
home from the park
on *that* lovely happy sunny summer day.

The end

sniff!
sniff!

WOOF!
WOOF!